SPIDER WOMAN

Anne Cameron

Illustrations by Nelle Olsen

HARBOUR PUBLISHING CO. LTD.

Text © Anne Cameron 1988
Illustrations © Nelle Olsen 1988
Cover and Book Design by Gaye Hammond
ISBN 0-920080-73-1

Harbour Publishing Co. Ltd.
Box 219, Madeira Park, B.C.
Canada   V0N 2H0

Canadian Cataloguing in Publication Data

Cameron, Anne, 1938—
    Spider woman

    ISBN 0-920080-73-1

    1. Indians of North America—Northwest Coast of North
America—Legends—Juvenile literature. I.Olsen, Nelle.   II.
Title.
PS8555.A43S6 1988   j398.2'089970795
        C88-091122-0

Printed and bound in Canada

10   9   8   7   6   5   4

When I was growing up on Vancouver Island I met a woman who was a storyteller. She shared many stories with me, and later, gave me permission to share them with others.

This woman's name was KLOPINUM. In English her name means "Keeper of the River of Copper." It is to her this book is dedicated, and it is in the spirit of sharing, which she taught me, these stories are offered to all small children. I hope you will enjoy them as much as I did.

Anne Cameron

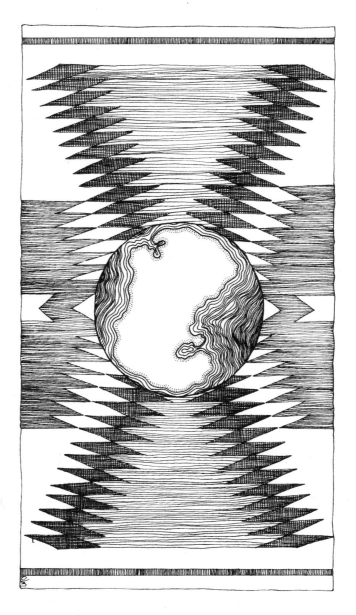

There was a time, long ago, when the world was not shaped as it is now. At that time there was only one huge flat piece of earth, floating in one huge ocean, and the ball that is the world was carefully fitted into its own hole in the blanket that is the sky.

At that time, Spider Woman lived in a land far to the south, a land of strange beauty where people walked on sand, under a sky that seldom knew rain.

Spider Woman lived under the sand in a huge web she had spun herself, and her children lived with her, listening to the happy sound of the lambs' hooves on their roof.

And then the earth began to shudder and quake, to split and crack, and Vancouver Island broke loose from the mainland and floated off, and sisters and brothers waved goodbye to each other sadly.

The world had begun to slip from its proper hole.

9

And through the gaps in the hole in the sky, the Birds of Torment began to appear. Until this time the people had known no pain, no sorrow, and no discomfort, for the Birds of Torment were unable to get past the world, but as the world began to slip the birds edged and inched through, and the people began to suffer terribly and cry bitterly.

Spider Woman heard the weeping. She left her many children in charge of her affairs, and climbed up the silver web-strand that leads from her house.

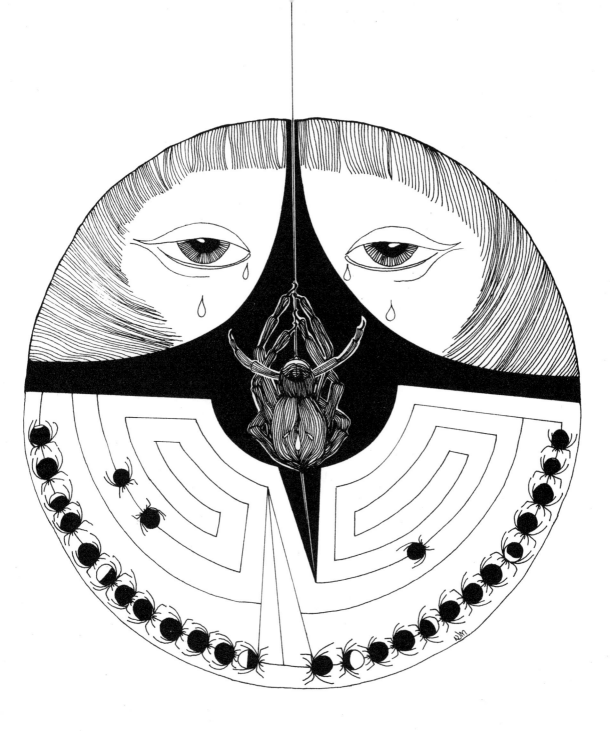

13

Spider Woman began to weave a net of silver around the slipping world, shooting strands of her webbing up to the moon, twisting and knotting the magic pattern that only she has ever been able to weave, and then she climbed up her own web-rope and stood on the moon, heaving and tugging, her sturdy little body straining and sweating.

When the world was almost in place again, Spider Woman took a section of rainbow and straightened it carefully, then wove a simple basket and fastened it to the end, and with this, the first Lacrosse stick, she caught the Birds of Torment as they flew through the sky, and one by one she stuffed them back through the hole to the place where they belonged.

The only ones she couldn't catch and force back into their proper place were the ones that brought tooth-ache, ear-ache, head-ache, and stomach-ache.

_____

Spider Woman pushed the earth into its proper place and tied the ends of her web securely. Some nights, when the moon is full and the clouds rolled away, you can see Spider Woman's web still cradling our world and holding us safe.

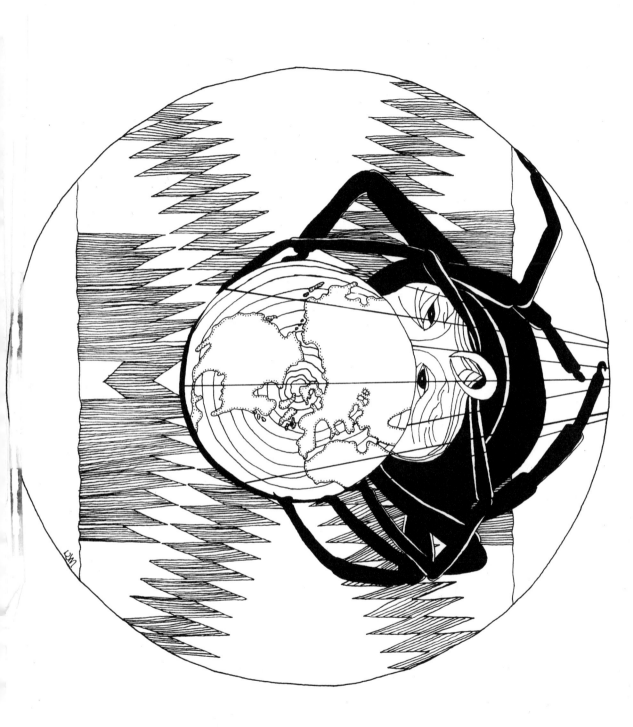

Then Spider Woman went to the tallest tree in all the world and explained her concerns. The tree willingly offered herself and became the pole Spider Woman placed under the earth to keep it steady.

To this very day you can see silver webs in the branches of trees, as the children of Spider Woman and the children of the big tree help each other; the trees provide a home for the spiders, the spiders catch the bugs that otherwise might infest and destroy the tree. When you see them, remember how the trees and spiders worked together to make this world a safe place for you to live.

When the world was safe, Spider Woman went back to her own land and the home she had fashioned under the sand, and she lived with her children where she could hear the patter of lambs' hooves on her roof, hear the sound of the flute the sheep herders played, and hear the songs and laughter of the women as they wove the wool into blankets and rugs.

BOOKS BY ANNE CAMERON

FOR CHILDREN

Raven Goes Berrypicking	$5.95 paper
Raven & Snipe	$5.95 paper
Spider Woman	$5.95 paper
Lazy Boy	$5.95 paper
Orca's Song	$5.95 paper
Raven Returns the Water	$5.95 paper
How the Loon Lost Her Voice	$5.95 paper
How Raven Freed the Moon	$5.95 paper
The Gumboot Geese	$9.95 paper

FOR ADULTS

Earth Witch	$5.95 paper
The Annie Poems	$7.95 paper
Dzelarhons: Myths of the Northwest Coast	$8.95 paper
Stubby Amberchuck & the Holy Grail	$19.95 cloth
Tales of the Cairds	$9.95 paper
South of an Unnamed Creek	$19.95 cloth
Women, Kids & Huckleberry Wine	$12.95 paper
Bright's Crossing	$12.95 paper
Escape to Beulah	$14.95 paper
Kick the Can	$14.95 paper
A Whole Brass Band	$16.95 paper

Available from Harbour Publishing,
Box 219, Madeira Park, BC, V0N 2H0
CANADA